THE BOXCAR CHILDREN®

SCHOOLHOUSE MYSTERY

Time to Read® is an early reader program designed to guide children to literacy success regardless of age or grade level. The program's three levels correspond to stages of reading readiness, making book selection straightforward, and assuring that when it's time for a child to read, the right book is waiting.

— Level — 1	Beginning to Read	• Large, simple type • Basic vocabulary	• Word repetition • Strong illustration support
— Level — 2	Reading with Help	• Short sentences • Engaging stories	• Simple dialogue • Illustration support
— Level — 3	Reading Independently	• Longer sentences • Harder words	• Short paragraphs • Increased story complexity

Library of Congress Cataloging-in-Publication data is on file with the publisher.

Copyright © 2021 by Albert Whitman & Company
First published in the United States of America
in 2021 by Albert Whitman & Company
ISBN 978-0-8075-7261-0 (hardcover)
ISBN 978-0-8075-7260-3 (ebook)
Printed in China
10 9 8 7 6 5 4 3 2 1 HH 26 25 24 23 22 21

Cover and interior art by Liz Brizzi

Visit The Boxcar Children® online at www.boxcarchildren.com.
For more information about Albert Whitman & Company,
visit our website at www.albertwhitman.com.

THE BOXCAR CHILDREN ®

SCHOOLHOUSE MYSTERY

Based on the book by
Gertrude Chandler Warner

Albert Whitman & Company
Chicago, Illinois

On a warm June day, the Aldens talked about what to do next on their summer vacation.

Benny had an idea.

"My friend says nothing exciting ever happens in Port Elizabeth. I want to go there."

Violet giggled.

"You want to go to Port Elizabeth because nothing happens there?" she asked.

Benny shook his head.

"I want to see what *does* happen. Something exciting happens every place; you just have to know where to look!"

Henry, Jessie, Violet, and Benny
loved going on adventures.
For a while they had lived
in a boxcar in the forest.
The children had many
adventures in the boxcar.

Then Grandfather found them.
Now they had a real home,
and they still had plenty of
adventures.

The children all agreed.
Their next adventure would be
to Port Elizabeth.
They left the very next morning.

"You can only get to the island
by day," Grandfather said.
"At night, the tide comes in.
It covers up the road!"

On the island, the Aldens
checked into the hotel.
Then they went for a walk.
They passed an old schoolhouse.
The door was open, but no one
was inside.

They came to a library.
The shelves were full of books.
But there was no librarian.
"Maybe nothing really does
happen here," Benny said.
"There are no people!"

Next, they went to the beach.

Jessie and Benny searched for seashells.

Henry read his book.

Violet painted the sand dunes.

The Aldens had no problem
finding fun on their own.
But when Violet looked up,
she saw that they were not
alone at all!

The girl's name was Marie,
and the boy was named Hal.
They were both shy at first.
Then Violet asked Marie
if she wanted to paint.

Hal showed Benny and Jessie
how to find the best shells.
By the end of the day, the
children were like old friends.

Jessie asked where the other children on the island were.

Marie explained that most of the children were shy.

Lots of visitors came to the island, but they didn't always care about the people in town.

Even their schoolteachers only stayed a little while.

"I never learned to paint in school," said Marie.

"Thanks for teaching me, Violet."

That gave Jessie an idea.
"Why don't we meet at the old
schoolhouse tomorrow?
We can learn from each other
some more!"

The next morning, the Aldens
ran to the schoolhouse.
There wasn't much inside.
The desks were empty.
The shelves were bare.
But Henry set out his books.

Violet arranged her paints.
Jessie and Benny laid out
their seashells.
And the children had all they
needed for their very own school.

When Benny rang the school
bell, it wasn't just Hal and
Marie who came.
Children from across the island
crowded into the schoolhouse.
Henry read stories.

Violet and Marie taught painting.
And Jessie and Benny shared
their seashells to make crafts.
"I like having our own school,"
Marie told Violet.

At recess, Grandfather arrived
with food for everyone.
Then a red car pulled up.

It was strange to see such a
fancy car on the little island.
"Who is that?" Benny asked.

"That is the Money Man,"
Hal explained.
"He comes each summer.
He trades money for old things."
The children crowded around.
Just like Hal said, the man
paid five dollars for a boy's
old quarter.
He bought Marie's old doll for
ten dollars.

"Why would someone trade ten dollars for an old doll?" asked Violet.

Henry explained that some old things are antiques.

If they are rare, they can be worth much more.

Violet nodded.

Still, she wondered about her friend's trade.

At the end of the day, the
Aldens found the key to the old
schoolhouse, locked up,
and went back to the hotel.
On the way, they passed the
Money Man's fancy red car.

"The road off of the island will be closed soon," Jessie said.

"I hope he doesn't get stuck."

"Maybe he will stay at the hotel," said Violet.

But that night, no one checked in to the little hotel.

The next morning, the red car was still parked on the street. At the schoolhouse, the Aldens noticed other strange things. Benny found chips of paint under the window. Violet found scratch marks on the shelves. "These weren't here yesterday," she said.

At recess, Henry went to
the library.
He found many good books,
but he noticed something was
different from his first visit.
The shelves were not as full.
Henry found the check-out log.
No one had checked out a
single book.
Had someone stolen books
from the library?

That evening, the Aldens ate supper on the beach.

The Money Man came up.

He offered to pay fifty dollars for Grandfather's watch.

Fifty dollars seemed like a lot to the children.

But Grandfather shook his head.

After the man had gone, Grandfather told them his watch was worth five times that much!

"I think that man is tricking people," Violet said.

She worried about those
who traded with him,
including Marie.

On the way back to the hotel,
Henry told the others about the
missing books in the library.
Could the Money Man have
taken the books to sell?
They had to find out.

The Aldens found the red car on
the street, but no Money Man.
"The tide is coming in," said
Jessie, "so he must be on the
island somewhere."
"We need to find him before
he gets away!" said Violet.
Benny knew just where to look.

The door to the schoolhouse was locked, but the window was open. It was the same window where Benny had found the paint chips. He knew someone had used it! Inside, they saw the Money Man.

He was opening a secret space behind the bookshelves! "That is why there were marks on the shelves!" said Violet.

Henry unlocked the door, and Grandfather led the children in. The man had taken out piles of antiques and stacks of books. "Those are the books from the library!" said Henry.

"And we know you've been
tricking people," said Violet.
The Money Man sighed.
He knew he was caught.
"I think it's time to make
things right," said Grandfather.

The next day, that's just what the Aldens did.

Henry brought the stolen books back to the library.

Grandfather returned people's antiques, including Marie's doll.

And the fancy red car left Port Elizabeth for good.

Soon it was time for the Aldens to leave too.

"I knew something exciting would happen here," said Benny.

"Like I said: you can find an adventure in every place…"

"And a chance to help others,"
Violet added.
"You just have to know where
to look."

Keep reading with the Boxcar Children!

Henry, Jessie, Violet, and Benny used to live in a boxcar. Now they have adventures everywhere they go! Adapted from the beloved chapter book series, these early readers allow kids to begin reading with the stories that started it all.

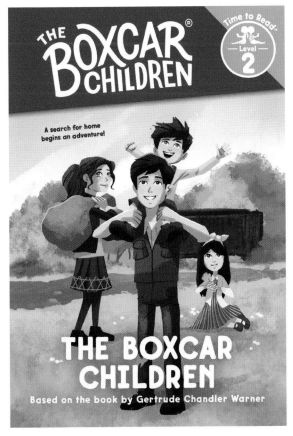

HC 978-0-8075-0839-8 · US $12.99
PB 978-0-8075-0835-0 · US $4.99

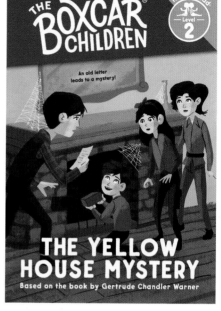

THE BOXCAR CHILDREN
Time to Read. Level 2

Four children.
One island.
Endless adventure.

SURPRISE ISLAND

Based on the movie *Surprise Island*
Based on the book by Gertrude Chandler Warner

HC 978-0-8075-7675-5 · US $12.99
PB 978-0-8075-7679-3 · US $4.99

THE BOXCAR CHILDREN
Time to Read. Level 2

An old letter
leads to a mystery!

THE YELLOW HOUSE MYSTERY

Based on the book by Gertrude Chandler Warner

HC 978-0-8075-9367-7 · US $12.99
PB 978-0-8075-9370-7 · US $4.99

THE BOXCAR CHILDREN
Time to Read. Level 2

Aunt Jane's ranch
has a big secret!

MYSTERY RANCH

Based on the book by Gertrude Chandler Warner

HC 978-0-8075-5402-9 · US $12.99
PB 978-0-8075-5435-7 · US $3.99

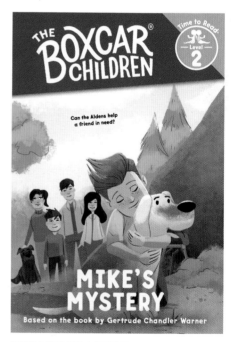

THE BOXCAR CHILDREN
Time to Read. Level 2

Can the Aldens help
a friend in need?

MIKE'S MYSTERY

Based on the book by Gertrude Chandler Warner

HC 978-0-8075-5142-4 · US $12.99
PB 978-0-8075-5139-4 · US $3.99

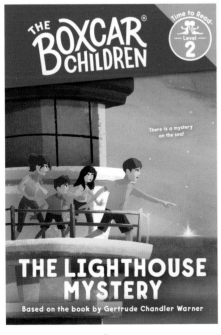

THE BOXCAR CHILDREN®
Time to Read. Level 2

The Aldens are on a tropical adventure!

BLUE BAY MYSTERY
Based on the book by Gertrude Chandler Warner

HC 978-0-8075-0795-7 · US $12.99
PB 978-0-8075-0800-8 · US $3.99

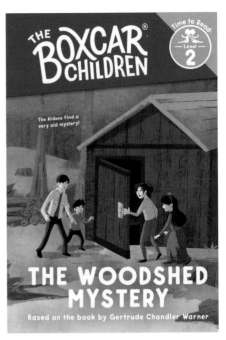

THE BOXCAR CHILDREN®
Time to Read. Level 2

The Aldens find a very old mystery!

THE WOODSHED MYSTERY
Based on the book by Gertrude Chandler Warner

HC 978-0-8075-9210-6 · US $12.99
PB 978-0-8075-9216-8 · US $3.99

THE BOXCAR CHILDREN®
Time to Read. Level 2

There is a mystery on the sea!

THE LIGHTHOUSE MYSTERY
Based on the book by Gertrude Chandler Warner

HC 978-0-8075-4548-5 · US $12.99
PB 978-0-8075-4552-2 · US $4.99

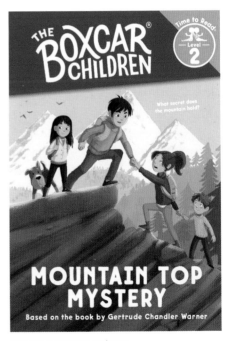

THE BOXCAR CHILDREN®
Time to Read. Level 2

What secret does the mountain hold?

MOUNTAIN TOP MYSTERY
Based on the book by Gertrude Chandler Warner

HC 978-0-8075-5291-9 · US $12.99
PB 978-0-8075-5289-6 · US $4.99

GERTRUDE CHANDLER WARNER discovered when she was teaching that many readers who like an exciting story could find no books that were both easy and fun to read. She decided to try to meet this need, and her first book, *The Boxcar Children*, quickly proved she had succeeded.

Miss Warner drew on her own experiences to write the mystery. As a child she spent hours watching trains go by on the tracks opposite her family home. She often dreamed about what it would be like to set up housekeeping in a caboose or freight car—the situation the Alden children find themselves in.

While the mystery element is central to each of Miss Warner's books, she never thought of them as strictly juvenile mysteries. She liked to stress the Aldens' independence and resourcefulness and their solid New England devotion to using up and making do. The Aldens go about most of their adventures with as little adult supervision as possible— something else that delights young readers.

Miss Warner lived in Putnam, Connecticut, until her death in 1979. During her lifetime, she received hundreds of letters from girls and boys telling her how much they liked her books.